Weekly Reader Presents

The Case of
the Missing Socks

By Rebecca Grand · Pictures by Jeffrey Severn

Muppet Press
Henry Holt and Company
NEW YORK

Copyright © 1984 by Henson Associates, Inc.
Fraggle Rock, Fraggles, Muppets, and character names are trademarks of Henson Associates, Inc.
All rights reserved, including the right to reproduce this
book or portions thereof in any form.
Published by Henry Holt and Company,
521 Fifth Avenue, New York, New York 10175

Library of Congress Cataloging in Publication Data

Grand, Rebecca.
The case of the missing socks.
Summary: Wembley and Boober, two Fraggle friends,
set out to catch the mysterious thief who is stealing
Boober's socks.
[1. Hosiery—Fiction. 2. Puppets—Fiction.
3. Mystery and detective stories] I. Severn,
Jeffrey, ill. II. Title.
PZ7.G7658Cas 1986   [E]   85-18958
ISBN: 0-03-007239-5

Printed in the United States of America

The Case of the Missing Socks

"SUFFERING socks!"

Wembley heard the scream and dropped the Doozer stick he was holding. His fur stood on end. Someone was yelling, and it sounded like Boober!

Wembley looked around, but there was no Boober in sight. *I'd better go see what's wrong,* he thought. So he ran off toward Boober's cave.

When he got there, the first thing he saw was Boober. The second thing he saw was Boober's clothesline. On the clothesline, as usual, were Boober's socks.

Boober, who was usually blue, was looking sort of red. He was staring at one of the socks on the line, and he seemed very annoyed.

"What's the matter?" Wembley asked. "I heard you yell."

"It's happened again," Boober said angrily. "Someone's stealing them! I'm sure of it!"

"Stealing what?" Wembley asked.

"Stealing my socks. Every morning I come to take my socks down off the line, and every morning one sock is missing."

"That's impossible!" Wembley said. "Fraggles never steal!"

"It's not impossible," Boober retorted. "Look!" He pointed to an empty space in the even row of socks. One of them was definitely missing.

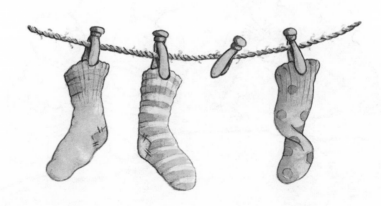

A Fraggle stealing anything was about as difficult to imagine as a Doozer going swimming. But the sock was gone.

"What are you going to do?" asked Wembley.

"I'm going to catch whoever it is," Boober said. "I'm going to build a trap for a sock thief."

"Can I help?" Wembley asked politely. He was a very helpful Fraggle.

"I guess so," Boober said grimly. "Unless you're the one who's been stealing my socks."

"Boober!" Wembley cried.

"I'm sorry," Boober muttered. "I don't know what's gotten into me. I'm just so upset!"

"That's okay, Boober," said Wembley. "We'll find out what's been happening to your socks together."

So Wembley joined Boober in collecting the sticks and strings and other things needed to build the trap.

"Wouldn't it be easier just to watch the socks until someone decided to steal one?" Wembley asked as they worked.

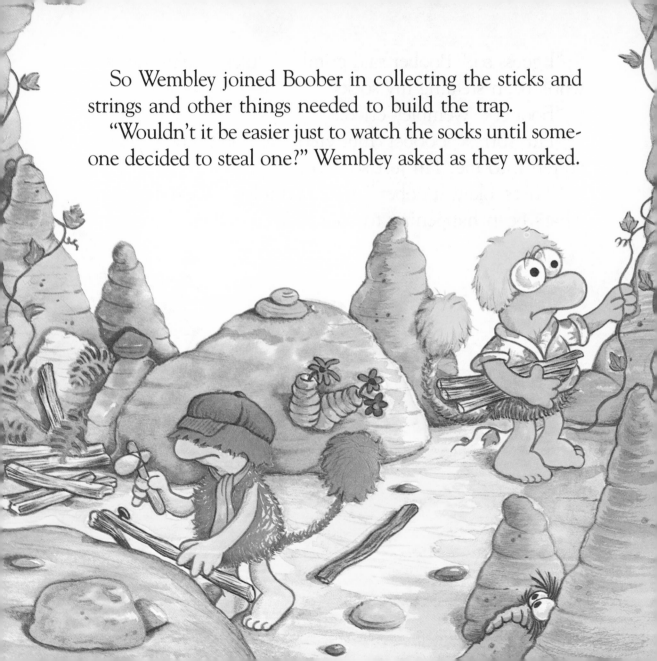

"It might," Boober said. "But I don't intend to be any-where near here when the thief appears. After all, I have my health to think of!"

It took Boober and Wembley all day, but finally the trap was finished.

Wembley and Boober lay awake in the dark, waiting for the sock thief to strike. As they lay there, Wembley started thinking. "Boober," he asked, "why do you suppose only one sock is stolen every night?"

"I have no idea," Boober said grumpily.

"Maybe it's not a Fraggle who's stealing your socks," Wembley went on. "Maybe it's a Horrible One-Footed Hopping Something-or-Other!"

"I hadn't thought of that," said Boober, wishing that Wembley hadn't thought of it either.

"Or maybe"—Wembley was just warming up—"it's a Big Blue-Nosed Grooble looking for a nose warmer. It's enough to curl your tail just thinking about it!"

It was more than enough to curl Boober's tail. In fact, it tied his tail into an unusually big knot.

Suddenly there was a noise. The trap had sprung!

Boober and Wembley looked at each other. "Maybe," Wembley began, "we'd better forget the whole thing."

Boober shook his head. "Absolutely not," he said. "Under normal circumstances, I can be as terrified as any other Fraggle. I can actually be *more* terrified. But those are my socks!" With that, he jumped out of bed.

Wembley couldn't let Boober go alone, so he got up, too. But when they got to the trap, it was empty—and another sock was missing!

"Well," Wembley said, "I guess we're too late! Can we go
back now?"

"Shhh!" Boober said, holding up his hand. "Do you hear
something?" There was a strange fluttering, rustling noise
in a tunnel ahead of them.

"That must be the thief!" whispered Boober. "Follow that sound!"

And follow it they did—up and down and around and, finally, out of Fraggle Rock and into the wilds of the Gorgs' Garden.

"Do we have to do this?" asked Wembley. "It's very dark out here."

"I have to save my socks!" Boober said. "Even if something evil or terrible has taken them—which it probably has!"

Wembley had never seen Boober be so brave. As a matter of fact, he had never seen Boober brave at all. Boober was usually a terrible coward. But he loved his laundry, and love is often stronger than fear.

And since Wembley loved Boober, he followed.

The Gorgs' Garden seemed to grow darker and darker. The sound of the wind in the trees turned into whispery laughter. Stones rose up from the ground to trip them, and the tall grass reached to grab them. Yet brave Boober and Wembley followed the fluttering noise that would lead them to Boober's socks—or so they hoped.

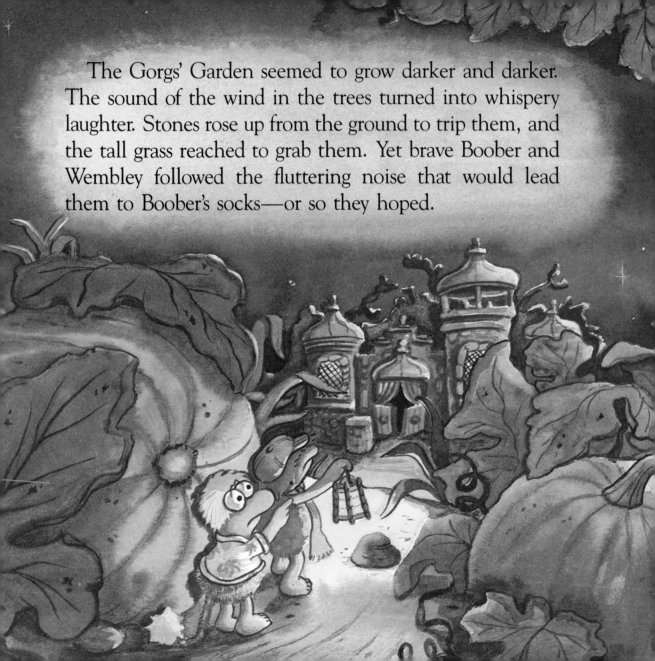

Finally they stopped in front of a large tree.

"That's where it lives," said Boober, looking up. The tree was huge. Its branches reached so high that neither Fraggle could tell where the tree ended and the sky began.

"Now what?" Wembley asked.

Without a word, Boober started to climb.

"You know," Wembley said, climbing up after him, "whatever's up there probably can't be as bad as the things we've been imagining."

"It's probably worse," Boober answered. "But I don't care. It has my socks!"

The two friends climbed and climbed. They climbed so high that they could barely see the ground. They finally reached the topmost branches of the giant tree.

That was when they saw *it* for the first time.

"It's . . . it's a little flutterbug!" cried Boober, almost falling out of the tree. "So this is where they live!"

"And there are your socks!" Wembley breathed. "I guess flutterbugs like socks as much as you do."

"No," said Boober gently, "look again."

Wembley did, and what he saw made him start to smile.

Five of Boober's socks were hanging from a branch, all in a row. Inside each one was a tiny baby flutterbug being rocked to sleep by the night breeze.

Without another word, Boober and Wembley climbed down the tree again. The garden had become a very different place. The trees and the grasses gently swayed, almost as if the whole world was rocking itself to a deep and peaceful sleep.

"You know," Boober said as they climbed in the hole to Fraggle Rock, "if you're not afraid to go looking, sometimes you can find something worth looking for."

The mystery was solved. But after that, there was a new
mystery in Fraggle Rock. Every once in a while, Boober
would leave just a single sock on his clothesline. None of
the other Fraggles knew why.

And Boober and Wembley weren't telling.